***Pra**_____ooks*

I got all _____ ristmas
and I jus _____ oking at
the pictures while I read to see what time they are in
and what they are wearing. My three favorites so far
are *Secret of the Prince's Tomb*, *Surprise at Yorktown*,
and *Challenge on the Hill of Fire*.

—Katie, age 8, Arbela, Missouri

*Surprise at Yorktown* is another great Adventures in
Odyssey story for kids to enjoy. It sweeps you into the
action and keeps you reading to find out who Beth
and Patrick can trust in dangerous times.

—Beth M., Elgin (IL) Children's Literature Examiner

After you start this book, you don't want to set it
down. The author keeps the action fast-paced and
moving, and there isn't really a slow spot unless
something mysterious is going on. It's a cool book.

—Nathan, age 17, longtime-AIO-fan, Elgin, Illinois

### More praise for *The Imagination Station® books*

I like the part where cannons are shooting. Why don't they make a movie of this? It would be awesome!

—Zachary, age 9, Forest City, North Carolina

A wonderful series of books weaving a bit of history, life skills, and biblical principles into encouraging and entertaining stories that are family friendly.

—Terri F., children's author and mom, Nashville, Ind.

*Surprise at Yorktown* is a wonderful mix of history, adventure, and fun! I highly recommend it for teaching Christian values as well. I look forward to reading other books in the series!

—Rona S., children's writer, Philadelphia, Penn.

*Surprise at Yorktown* was exciting and fun to read. I liked seeing what it might have been like to live during the American Revolution.

—Will, age 8, Lexington, Kentucky

FOCUS ON THE FAMILY PRESENTS

# Surprise at Yorktown

**BOOK 15**

**MARIANNE HERING • NANCY I. SANDERS**
**CREATIVE DIRECTION BY PAUL MCCUSKER**
**ILLUSTRATED BY DAVID HOHN**

TYNDALE

FOCUS ON THE FAMILY • ADVENTURES IN ODYSSEY®
TYNDALE HOUSE PUBLISHERS, INC. • CAROL STREAM, ILLINOIS

*Surprise at Yorktown*
© 2014 Focus on the Family

ISBN: 978-1-58997-776-1

A Focus on the Family book published by Tyndale House Publishers, Inc., Carol Stream, Illinois 60188.

Focus on the Family and Adventures in Odyssey, and the accompanying logos and designs, are federally registered trademarks, and The Imagination Station is a federally registered trademark of Focus on the Family, 8605 Explorer Drive, Colorado Springs, CO 80920.

*TYNDALE* and Tyndale's quill logo are registered trademarks of Tyndale House Publishers, Inc.

With the exception of known historical figures, all characters are the product of the authors' imaginations.

Cover design by Michael Heath | Magnus Creative

For Library of Congress Cataloging-in-Publication Data for this title, visit http://www.loc.gov.

Printed in the United States of America

3 4 5 6 7 8 9 / 19 18 17 16 15

For manufacturing information regarding this product, please call 1-800-323-9400.

To Josiah,

Ben's youngest brother-in-law of awesomeness.

May God be with you as you go through life's

"Adventures." Maybe some New Year's Eve I'll beat

you at Pit. (Watch out for the Bear!)

—NIS

# Contents

# *Prologue*

Whit's End is an old house in the town of Odyssey. It has an ice-cream shop on the main floor. And it has a workshop downstairs.

Mr. Whittaker owns Whit's End. He is kind but also mysterious. He often works at the ice-cream shop. He also likes to invent things in his workshop. One of his favorite inventions is the Imagination Station.

The Imagination Station lets kids travel to

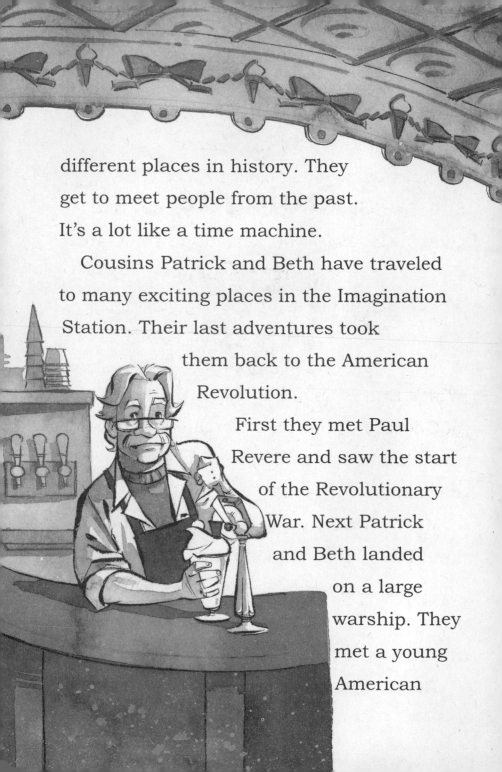

different places in history. They get to meet people from the past. It's a lot like a time machine.

Cousins Patrick and Beth have traveled to many exciting places in the Imagination Station. Their last adventures took them back to the American Revolution.

First they met Paul Revere and saw the start of the Revolutionary War. Next Patrick and Beth landed on a large warship. They met a young American patriot named James Forten. He risked his life to fight at sea for his country.

The cousins came back to Whit's End. Still, Patrick was disappointed. They had gone to the American Revolution twice. But they never met George Washington. So Whit promised to send them on another adventure.

Patrick and Beth could hardly wait to go!

But they had no idea what they were going to face.

# *The Workshop*

Beth and Patrick raced each other to Whit's End. They hurried to the basement.

The Imagination Station sat in the center of the vast workroom. The machine looked like the front part of a helicopter. The doors on each side stood open.

The cousins rushed to get inside the Imagination Station.

"I get to push the red button," Patrick cried.

"Not if I get there first," Beth said. She jumped over a broken TV to move ahead of Patrick.

"Whoa!" Mr. Whitaker said. He held up his hand to signal them to stop.

The cousins slowed down.

"But we're ready to go," Patrick said.

Mr. Whittaker stood next to his workbench. "Aren't you forgetting something?" he asked.

Patrick thought a minute. "Please?" he said.

Mr. Whittaker chuckled. "Saying 'please' is a good thing," he told them. "But that isn't what I meant."

"Our gifts!" Beth said.

"That's right," Whit said. *Gifts* is the word they used for the things Whit gave them for their adventures. The gifts helped the cousins in times of need.

Whit's workbench was cluttered with all kinds of things. Beth saw a hammer and several screwdrivers. Bits of wire and tiny springs were scattered all over.

Whit lifted up a white cloth from the workbench. Underneath was a long, thin object.

Beth gasped with delight. "Is that a fife?" she asked.

"Yes, it is," Whit said. He placed the fife in Beth's hands.

"I have a recorder at home," Beth said. "I learned to play 'Yankee Doodle' on it."

Patrick shook his head and said, "What's the difference between a fife and a recorder? They look the same to me."

"The fife is a simple wood flute," Mr. Whittaker said. "It's held sideways. The recorder is held longways. And it has a full

6

mouthpiece."

"Why did the Continental army use a fife for marching?" Beth asked.

"The fife was easy to carry and use," Mr. Whittaker said.

Beth held the fife to her lips. She blew across the mouth hole. A soft, high whistle came out. She moved her fingers across the finger holes and slowly played "Yankee Doodle."

"Very good," Whit said.

Whit handed the white cloth to Patrick.

"What's this?" Patrick asked.

"It's a handkerchief," Whit said. "People used these before paper tissues were invented."

"You mean to blow their noses in?" Patrick asked, wrinkling his nose. "Eww. Gross." He carefully lifted the handkerchief between his thumb and pointer finger.

"Don't worry," Whit said with a chuckle. "It's clean."

Beth thought Patrick's handkerchief was an unusual gift. She wondered why she had been given a fife. She wanted to ask but knew she would find out in time.

"Can we go?" Patrick asked.

"*May* we?" Beth said, correcting her cousin.

Beth knew Patrick wanted to meet George Washington. She did too.

Whit nodded. "The program is ready," he said. "Just push the red button."

Beth sat down in the Imagination Station again. Patrick sat next to her. The doors slid closed with a soft *swoosh*.

Beth held one hand over the large red button on the dashboard. She felt a familiar thrill bubbling up inside. "*May* I?" Beth asked Patrick.

"Yes, you *can*," Patrick said.

Beth laughed. Then she punched the red button.

The machine rumbled and shook.

Beth's seat jiggled underneath her. She closed her eyes. She felt like Alice in Wonderland. She was falling down, down, down a deep, dark hole.

The machine jerked. The rumble grew louder.

The Imagination Station whirled.

Suddenly, everything went black.

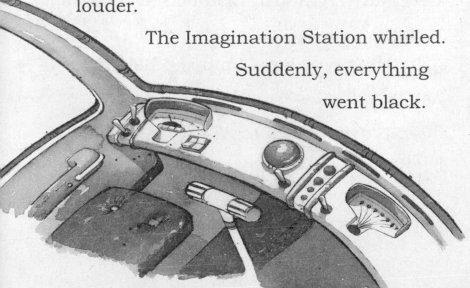

# *Laundry Day*

A cool breeze swept over Patrick. He opened his eyes. He and Beth were high up in a tree. Patrick grabbed a branch to keep from falling.

Beth sat on a large limb and held tight to a branch above her head. The tree's red-and-orange leaves told Patrick it was fall.

The hum of the Imagination Station faded.

Patrick swung his legs back and forth. He was wearing a white shirt under a blue jacket. It had two rows of shiny buttons. His pants looked like long shorts. Long stockings led down to brown leather shoes.

Patrick stuffed the white handkerchief inside his jacket pocket. Then he reached up to touch his hat. It was made of felt and shaped like a triangle.

Patrick looked at Beth.

She wore a long red dress. It had white ruffles around the sleeves. A long white apron covered the front of her dress. Beth slipped her fife into the apron's large pocket.

"We're wearing the same clothes we wore in our last two adventures," Patrick said.

Beth nodded.

A *boom* suddenly filled the silence.

The cousins rocked in the tree.

"A cannon!" Patrick cried.

"And it isn't very far away," Beth said as

she peered through the leaves.

Patrick smelled gunpowder. He pushed a branch away from his face and peeked out. White clouds mingled with wisps of gray smoke. He looked beyond the nearby woods. Cannons and tents spread across a grassy field.

"We're near a battlefield," Patrick said. "But which one?"

A wide river glinted in the sun beyond the field. Boats with tall sails floated on the water.

Beth asked, "Can you tell if the ships are British or American?"

Patrick squinted his eyes. He hoped to see the flags. But the ships were too far away.

"What are you doing up there?" a girl's voice asked from below them.

Patrick looked down.

A teen girl stood looking up at them. She wore a ruffled white cap. A blonde curl had slipped out and hung down her face. She glared at the cousins with her hands on her hips.

The girl stamped her foot. "Come down from there!" she said.

Patrick looked at Beth. She shrugged.

Patrick scrambled down through the branches. He jumped from the last branch to the ground. He reached up to help his cousin.

Beth began to climb down slowly. She was careful to keep her dress from snagging on a branch.

Patrick turned to face the girl. "Here we are," he said.

The girl was wearing a long brown dress. The front of it was white. The bottom half of

her sleeves were white too.
A long white apron was tied
around her waist.

"Who are you?" the girl asked.

"My name is Patrick. And this is my cousin Beth," Patrick said.

"My name is Sally," the girl said. She studied the cousins for a minute. Then she curtsied. "Were you sent from the town?"

"We're from *a* town," Patrick said. He knew better than to try to explain about Whit's End or the Imagination Station.

"Then you may help me deliver the laundry," Sally said.

"Laundry?" Beth asked.

"Yes," Sally said. "My mother and I take care of the general's laundry. All the clean clothes and linens need to be carried to his headquarters."

Sally motioned toward nearby bushes. Several white shirts and sheets were spread out over the shrubs to dry.

The word *general* gave Patrick hope that he might finally meet George Washington. "We'll be glad to help you," Patrick said. "Won't we, Beth?"

"Sure," Beth said, giving Patrick a knowing glance. Her look told Patrick she was thinking the same thing he was.

Sally smiled and nodded. She led the cousins to the bushes and showed them how to gather the laundry in large white sheets. They tied the sheet corners to form three big bundles.

Patrick lifted up his bundle and hefted it over his shoulder. He could smell the laundry's sun-warmed freshness.

Sally and Beth carried their loads in front of them.

Patrick followed the girls through the woods. They were talking, but Patrick wasn't listening. His mind was on meeting the future first president of the United States, General George Washington.

# The Dark Cave

Sally led Patrick and Beth out of the woods. They came to the edge of the wide river.

A steep cliff rose to one side. It blocked their view of the field.

*Boom! Boom! Boom!* The cannon blasts had started again. They were closer now. *Too close,* Patrick thought. He tightened his grip around the bundle of laundry.

"Are we heading *toward* the cannons?" he asked Sally.

The girl looked at him as if he'd asked a silly question. "You'll head toward the cannons no matter which direction you go," she said. "The two sides are getting closer and closer."

"Are we safe?" Beth asked.

"As safe as you'll be anywhere," Sally said.

Patrick was about to ask her where they were. But a nearby cannon startled him.

Sally crouched down. Patrick and Beth did the same.

They followed the girl along the river's edge.

B*oom!* Another cannon shot.

Sally quickly turned to the left. She led them away from the river. "It's too dangerous to be out in the open," she called.

Patrick had to agree.

Sally ducked into a cave. It was hidden in the side of the cliff.

Patrick hesitated. It looked like the entrance to a mine.

Sally motioned for the cousins to come inside. "The troops dug these shelters to hide in," she said.

Beth stepped inside. Patrick followed.

They entered a large, dark dugout. Green cloth hung against the walls like curtains. Water dripped from cracks in the rock ceiling. Small puddles formed on the dirt floor. The air smelled moldy and damp.

Folding trays stood in the center of the cave. They were covered with papers, bottles of ink, quill pens, and several lanterns. Patrick saw an army cot back in the darkest corner. Large trunks had been set around the front edge of the cave. The floor was covered with wood slats.

Sally put down her bundle of laundry.

She picked up a clean white shirt and opened one of the trunks. She folded the shirt and placed it in the trunk.

"Be quick now," she said. "The general may return at any moment. We mustn't get in his way."

Beth and Patrick both lowered their bundles. They helped put away the laundry.

Just then Patrick heard men's voices. He caught his breath.

Sally waved for them to hurry up and finish packing the laundry.

A deep voice said, "Spread the word. We will escape at midnight."

"If the weather is good," another voice said.

Three men walked into the cave.

Patrick gasped. The men were all wearing red coats. These weren't American soldiers. They were British!

# Redcoats

Patrick and Beth looked wide-eyed at each other. They were in enemy territory!

The three men wore white shirts under their red coats. Their white pants were tucked into tall black boots. Their hair hung loosely under their large black hats.

They paid no attention to the children. The man with the deep voice leaned over one of the trays. He unrolled a map on top of the papers. "Look here," he said.

The other men leaned close to see the map. One of them said, "With respect, General Cornwallis, we have only a few ships. We can't transport all the men."

Patrick put a hand over his mouth to keep from gasping. General Cornwallis was one of George Washington's greatest enemies.

General Cornwallis tapped the map with his finger. "I have sent word to our commander at Gloucester Point," he said. "He has small boats that he will bring across the river to us after dark."

"You wish to retreat?" the officer asked.

Cornwallis frowned and said, "We've nearly run out of shells, Officer Mudge. We have little food left. This siege has lasted far too long. We must cross the river."

"Is there no hope of help from the north?" Officer Mudge asked. "Surely General Clinton

is sending ships and troops from New York."

"I have written to the general not to come," General Cornwallis said.

Officer Mudge looked surprised.

"It would be folly for them to help us now," Cornwallis said. "We must use our own wits to fool the Americans."

"How will we fool them?" Officer Mudge asked.

"I will write a letter to General Washington. It will say that I am ready to surrender," Cornwallis said. "I will stall him with the lie. They will stop their shelling while we talk. They will not be expecting us to slip away in the night."

"Are you truly prepared to give up Yorktown?" Officer Mudge asked.

*Yorktown!* Patrick knew that Yorktown was an important battleground in the

American Revolution. But he couldn't
remember the details.

"They will think it's a coward's way out,"
Officer Mudge said.

Cornwallis frowned at Mudge. "It is not
cowardly to free ourselves," he said sharply.
"It is not cowardly to set our own trap for
the Americans. It is not cowardly to win this
war."

*Achoo!* Officer Mudge suddenly sneezed.

He turned toward Sally. "Do you have a
clean pocket handkerchief, girl?" he said
sharply.

Patrick thought of the handkerchief Mr.
Whittaker had given to him. He was about to
offer it, but Sally stepped forward.

"Here, sir," Sally said in a small voice. She
held out a handkerchief in her hand.

Officer Mudge grabbed the cloth without

saying thank you. He blew his nose. The noise sounded like a trumpet blast. He stuffed the dirty handkerchief into his pocket.

Patrick was glad he hadn't wasted Whit's gift on Mudge's nose.

Suddenly a black man stepped into the cave. He had red pants tucked into knee-high brown boots. His white shirt had a ruffle at the neck. He wore a red jacket. His black hat was decorated with white-and-purple flowers.

The man carried a satchel with a long strap. It hung over his shoulder. A loaf of bread was tucked underneath one arm.

General Cornwallis looked up. "Come in, Armistead," he said. "Wait over there."

"Yes, sir," the man called Armistead said.

His voice was rich and deep. He stepped in and crossed to the other table. He stood straight and still like a statue.

"The boats will arrive before midnight," the general said to Officer Mudge. "I believe we could move most of our troops out before morning light. But we must be prepared and move quickly."

"Yes, General," Officer Mudge said.

Cornwallis turned to the second officer. "Give orders for the troops to get ready," he said. "They will soon board the Gloucester boats."

The second officer saluted. Then he turned and left the cave.

Sally curtsied to the general. "With your leave, sir, may we go?"

General Cornwallis kept his eyes on the map and waved to dismiss them.

Officer Mudge held up a hand. "Have you finished the laundry?" he asked Sally.

"Yes, sir."

"Then report to the docks," Officer Mudge said. "Tell the officer in charge, Colonel Lake, that I sent you. You three are to watch for stowaways."

Sally said, "But—

"But nothing," Officer Mudge said with a sneer. "Now, obey me or suffer."

"Yes, sir," Sally said, giving a curtsey.

As he left the cave, Patrick glanced back. The two officers and Armistead were looking at the map. Somehow he had to warn the Americans about General Cornwallis's plan. If the British escaped now, it could change the end of the war.

But how could he and Beth get away?

# Working for King George

Beth, Patrick, and Sally left the cave and walked back the way they had come. Beth couldn't walk away fast enough. She knew that Patrick felt the same way she did. They had to find George Washington and tell him Cornwallis's plan. But she also knew she shouldn't say anything in front of Sally.

They reached the river's edge.

"Who was the man in the flowered hat?"

Beth asked. She tried to make the question sound natural.

"That was James Armistead," Sally said. "He's not wearing a uniform because he's a runaway slave. But now he's General Cornwallis's servant. Lots of slaves have run away and joined the British. They were promised freedom if the British win the war."

Beth remembered their adventure with another man named James—James Forten. He had refused to fight for the British.

Patrick gazed at the river. "Where exactly are we?" he asked.

"You don't know?" Sally said. She looked at him with suspicion. "I thought you came from town."

"He got turned around," Beth said. "Not all people are good with directions."

"Yorktown is to the north of us," Sally said.

Beth looked at Patrick. How could they stop the British from escaping?

"It's easy to get mixed up these days," Sally said as they walked on. "Nothing's the same since the British came. They've dug up the earth with trenches. The ground has been blasted with cannonballs. Now many of the rabbits and squirrels have run off."

"Are the British allowed to boss you around like that?" Beth asked.

Sally frowned. "The British are allowed to do whatever they want," she said. "Who's going to stop them?"

Sally now led them up the river again.

"What can we do?" Beth whispered to Patrick.

"I don't know," Patrick said.

*Boom! Boom! Boom!*

The cannon blasts sounded all around

them. After a few moments, they rounded the cliff wall.

Beth and Patrick now saw what the rock wall had blocked from view. British soldiers in bright-red jackets were everywhere. Injured soldiers lay on the ground. Their wounds were wrapped with dirty cloths. Other redcoats carried large packs.

Several wooden docks jutted out into the river. Tall ships sat near the docks. Their masts stood bare. The ships looked abandoned.

"Why don't they escape on those ships?" Beth asked.

Sally laughed. "The sails were stripped off to use as tents," she said. "They've taken as much wood as they can to build all the forts."

"Then why are we here?" Patrick asked.

Sally pointed to smaller boats bobbing

in the water. They were the size of lifeboats. Only a handful of people could fit into them. "Runaway slaves and British deserters have been stealing those," she said.

Facing the docks were rows of buildings and stores. Barrels, broken crates, and trash could be seen in the long shadows on the street.

*Boom! Boom! Boom!*

The sound of more cannons continued in the background.

Sally approached a soldier standing guard on the docks. "Sir? Are you Colonel Lake?" she asked.

The soldier frowned. "What do you want?"

"Officer Mudge ordered me to report to you," Sally said. "These children are here to serve you."

"I asked for a *guard* to stop stowaways,"

the guard said. "They're *children*."

"Yes, sir," Sally said. "Perhaps that's why Officer Mudge sent two."

*Only two?* Beth thought.

Sally curtsied to the soldier and turned away.

"Sally, wait!" Patrick called. "You're supposed to help too!"

Sally looked over her shoulder. "I've got to get the general his clean red clothes," she said. With that remark, she was gone.

Beth crossed her arms. "And we need to get back to our general too," Beth said. She was thinking about General Washington.

The soldier pressed his lips together. "Stop talking and follow me," he said. "You're working for King George tonight."

# A Miracle

Beth and Patrick followed Colonel Lake along a busy street. By now it was getting dark. Patrick looked around for a way of escape. It would be easier to hide after the sun had set.

Colonel Lake stopped near the river's edge. He pointed with his rifle toward a tall pile of baggage and crates.

"Hide behind there," the redcoat said. "And don't fall asleep. Call me if you see anyone getting into a boat."

Beth nodded.

"I won't fall asleep," Patrick said.

Colonel Lake narrowed his eyes. "I'll be keeping my eye on you two. No mischief!" The soldier lifted his rifle and moved a few feet away.

Patrick felt restless. He realized the cannons had stopped firing. It was quiet now and cooler.

Another soldier walked up to Colonel Lake. As the two men talked, Patrick crouched down. He used the moment to talk to Beth.

"Beth!" he said in a low voice. "C'mon! We have to get out of here. It's darker now. And Colonel Lake isn't watching."

Patrick scooted away and Beth followed. They ducked behind barrels and crates as best as they could. They stopped behind a wagon filled with supplies.

"How much farther till we're off the dock?" Beth whispered.

"Let me check," Patrick said. He leaned out from behind the wagon.

Just then, a strong hand covered Patrick's mouth. The other hand grabbed his shoulder.

Patrick tried to call out. He kicked at the man's bare feet and tried to twist away. But the man held on tight.

Patrick glanced at Beth. Another man held her captive too. His skin was very dark, and he was dressed in rags. Patrick wondered if both men were runaway slaves.

"We don't want to hurt anybody," the man said in Patrick's ear. "I'll let you talk if you promise not to cry out."

Patrick nodded. The rough hand over Patrick's mouth relaxed. Then Patrick twisted his head free.

"So what *do* you want?" Patrick asked.

The man was as big as a bear. He wore loose black pants and a white shirt.

"My name is Samuel," the man said. "And I want you to keep quiet. My friend here needs to get to a boat."

"I'm a lookout for the redcoats," Patrick said. "They'll shoot you if they see you."

"Ah, but you don't want to help the British, do you?" Samuel asked.

"How do you know that?" Patrick asked.

"You're not wearing a uniform," Samuel said. "And I saw you sneaking away from the guard."

Patrick thought about it. He looked carefully at the man holding Beth. "Your friend's clothes say he's a slave," Patrick said.

"That's true," Samuel said.

"Then help me get to George Washington," Patrick said, "and I won't say a word."

The man smiled and nodded. "Moses," he said to the man in rags. "Slip through the water now. Get on that boat double-quick."

The man called Moses let Beth go.

She looked wide-eyed at Patrick and took a deep breath. But she didn't scream.

Moses slipped out from behind the wagon and ran catlike to the water.

Patrick didn't know where the redcoat had gone. He expected shouts and gunfire. But all was silent except for a gentle splashing as Moses waded into the river. Patrick saw him swim into the growing darkness.

"You know they're watching for you," Patrick said to Samuel. "Why are you leaving tonight?"

"If the British leave, Moses' owner will come looking for him," Samuel said. "It will be worse than death. He likely wouldn't live through the first beating."

"Aren't you going?" Patrick asked.

"Me?" Samuel said. "I'm already free," He knelt low behind the wagon. "I'm here to help my friends. More slaves will be coming soon."

Patrick felt helpless as he watched Moses swim. Moses reached the nearest boat. He climbed over its side and disappeared from view. The boat bobbed and tipped. Then a pair of oars appeared. Moses sat up and quietly rowed the boat away.

"Best pray he makes it to freedom," Samuel said.

"Yes," Beth said. "But if he gets away in a boat, then so can each British soldier."

Patrick felt confused too. He didn't want the British soldiers to get away. But he wanted Moses and other slaves to escape.

"Are more stowaways coming?" Patrick asked Samuel.

"Yes, sir," the man said softly.

Patrick heard noises from farther down the dock. A large boat rowed by a handful of redcoats bumped up to the dock. Patrick guessed it was the first boat from the other side of the river. That meant the British soldiers could now escape one boat at a time.

"We didn't make it to General Washington in time," Patrick said. "Now General Cornwallis will escape."

"If the boats can cross the river, the British will get away," Beth said. "This war will never end. We need a miracle."

*A miracle*, Patrick thought. They hadn't been able to warn George Washington. What could stop the British now? Only a miracle. A glimmer of hope entered his heart.

Patrick remembered John Hancock and Samuel Adams. They had asked God for help when the Revolutionary War started. Now America needed God's help to bring the war to an end.

Patrick closed his eyes and bowed his head. He prayed, *Dear God, please stop the redcoats from escaping. Bring an end to the fighting.*

"What will the slaves do if the British leave?" Beth asked.

"The British aren't leaving," Samuel said.

"Why not?" Patrick asked.

Samuel smiled and said, "Because I prayed and I saw your friend pray. The good

Lord will hold the British back somehow."

"How will God stop them?" Patrick asked.

Just then lightning flashed across the sky.

The man laughed.

*Kaboom!* Thunder shook the barrels on the dock.

"Like that!" Samuel said. "My work is done. Sorry that I can't take you to General Washington. I have to warn the runaways. It's not safe for them to leave tonight."

"That's okay," Patrick said. "Stay safe."

Samuel nodded and then crept away. He vanished into the night.

*Whoosh!*—a gust of wind lifted Patrick's hat off his head. He grabbed it before it got far.

The redcoats scrambled around on the dock.

*Boom. KABOOM!* Another flash of lightning. Then another.

A Miracle

Suddenly rain poured down. Patrick
pressed his hat onto his head. It was little
protection against the pounding storm.

Each flash of lightning lit up the night.
Huge waves rose up on the river and
splashed up on the street. The British boats
looked like toys. They were being tossed
about by the waves.

*They're turning back!* Patrick thought.
*This storm is making it too dangerous for
them to escape!* His heart felt full of hope by
this answer to his prayer.

Lightning hit close by. Out of instinct, the
cousins leaped away from the wagon.

"Hurry," Patrick said. "Let's find
someplace safe to hide!"

Beth started to run. But she stumbled
and fell over her long dress.

Patrick bent to help her up. But strong

arms grabbed him first. It was Colonel Lake.

"I've been looking for you," the guard shouted. "You left your post!"

"It doesn't matter now," Patrick said. "No stowaways can get away in this storm!"

Colonel Lake looked at the waves. He let go of Patrick.

"Get out of the rain, then!" the guard shouted. "It's every man for himself now!"

"Where is it safe?" Patrick asked.

But the guard wasn't listening. He pushed away from Patrick. The man disappeared beyond the wall of rain.

Patrick turned around to find Beth.

She was gone.

# Armistead

*Kaboom!* Beth clapped her hands over her ears. Just then she saw Colonel Lake grab Patrick. She ducked into a nearby warehouse to escape. She opened the door a crack and peeked outside. It seemed safe. Then she stuck her head outside.

"Patrick!" Beth shouted. "Patrick, come this way!"

Beth saw a form moving toward the warehouse. But the rain made it difficult for her to see. Was it Patrick? The shape was the right height. It wore the right hat. And it was sopping.

She flung the door wide open. Patrick's form stepped inside. He took off his hat. Water spilled from its curved brim.

Beth shut the door quickly.

"What is this place?" Patrick asked.

"It must be a storage warehouse," Beth said. "It's got great stuff in here."

Beth found a brown wool blanket on a crate. She wrapped it around her. Then she pulled another one from the top of a barrel. "Here," she said, "this will warm you up."

Patrick thanked her and put the blanket around him. "Did you see what happened?" he asked. His eyes were huge with excitement. "God sent a storm so the British couldn't escape!"

"I hope Moses got across," Beth said. "Or that he can swim to safety."

"I'm sure he'll be fine," Patrick said. "He left before the waves got really rough."

*Boom. Kaboom!*

Patrick pulled the blanket tight around him. He sat down on the floor.

Beth sat down across from him. She leaned her back against the tall counter. She asked, "What should we do now?"

"It must be past midnight," Patrick said. "We should get some sleep."

"What about our escape?" she asked.

Patrick lay down on his side. "We can't go anywhere in this storm," he said.

"Will we ever find George Washington?" Beth asked.

"I hope so," Patrick said. He took off his jacket. He pulled off his shoes. Then he closed his eyes.

"Good night," Beth said. She took off her shoes.

"Good night," Patrick said in a sleepy voice.

Beth woke with a start. Her neck felt stiff. A gray dawn dimly lit a window.

Patrick sat next to her pulling on his shoes.

Beth stood up and stretched. She looked around the warehouse. She hoped she might discover something helpful in the daylight. "I'm hungry," she said.

Patrick stood up. "Me, too," he said. "But we've got to get away from the British as fast as we can."

Beth peeked out the door. "Most of the soldiers are down by the docks," she said. "The storm must have wrecked everything."

Beth listened for a moment. The cannons were silent. She saw a large square of paper on one of the barrels. She studied it closely. "Look!" she said. "It's a map of the area!"

Patrick joined her near the map.

The map was drawn by hand. It showed a path from the docks to the warehouses.

"It's a delivery map," Beth said.

"But look, Beth," Patrick said. "It also has danger areas marked."

Beth pointed to an *X* on the map. "This must be where we are now," she said. There was a line of buildings across from it. "I say we leave the docks *this* way. It should take us to the Americans."

"But look. That way goes across an open field," Patrick said. "We might get shot at or hit with cannonballs."

"What if we hide in these trees?" Beth asked,

53

pointing to another area of the map.

"We may find cover there," Patrick said. He grabbed the map and folded it up. Then he pushed it into his pocket. "Let's go while we can."

Beth and Patrick hurried out of the building. They turned a corner to slip behind the warehouses. Then they followed a small street away from the river.

Soldiers in bright-red jackets gathered at the edge of a dirt wall to the left. Sharp-pointed logs stuck out of it. "Not that way," Beth said.

The cousins headed toward the trees along the edge of the town. Soon they were in the woods. After several minutes, they came out the other side.

They faced a large open space. Forts made of dirt and large logs stood nearby.

Beth peered through gaps in the logs. She saw British soldiers moving wagons and horses.

"Look at the cannons," Patrick said. "They're all aimed at Yorktown. That's where the Americans are!"

"They're that close?" Beth asked. No wonder the cannons were so loud.

"How do we get to the other side without being shot by a stray bullet?" Beth asked.

Patrick pointed to deep holes in the ground. "Those were made by the cannonballs," he said. "We can run from one to the other all the way to the American line. Hurry!"

Patrick dashed away before Beth could say anything. She reluctantly ran after him.

Patrick led them across an open area of grass. Then they crouched inside one of the holes. It was so deep it hid them completely. Then they ran behind the wide trunk of a tall tree. Then they found another hole.

The cousins slowly made their way across the field. The American fort was now close. Their last stop was a wide boulder. They threw themselves behind it.

Beth gasped in surprise.

A man sat on the ground. He wore a black hat with white-and-purple flowers on it. In his hand was a tall boot. He was stuffing papers inside it.

He looked up at them with alarm.

Beth recognized him. It was the servant from the cave. General Cornwallis had called him Armistead.

Armistead glared at them. He asked, "What are you doing here?"

# 8

# *Lies?*

Patrick was panting hard from running. He crouched down next to Armistead.

Beth dropped to her knees next to Patrick.

Armistead continued to glare at them. He was waiting for an answer.

"We're trying to get to the American side," Patrick said.

"I saw you in General Cornwallis's cave," Armistead said. "What business do you have with the Americans?"

"We got lost," Beth said quickly. "We weren't supposed to be on the British side."

Armistead eyed them a moment. Then he calmly pulled his boot back on his foot.

"What are *you* doing here?" Patrick asked.

Armistead said, "I'm about to eat breakfast. Are you hungry?" He reached into a large white canvas bag on the ground next to him. He pulled out two red apples and held them out for the cousins.

"Thank you," the cousins both said.

Patrick bit into his with a loud crunch. It was sweet goodness. Beth loudly bit into hers.

"This is a strange place to have breakfast," Patrick said between bites.

Armistead shrugged his shoulders. "For some folks, maybe," he said. "But not for me. I gather supplies for the Continental army. I just picked a poke of apples. They're here in my haversack."

"You work for the Continental army?" Beth asked. "But you were with General Cornwallis."

The man smiled like a cat. He said, "My name is James Armistead. Who are you?"

The cousins told him their names.

Patrick was about to question Armistead. But cannon fire interrupted him. *The Americans were attacking the British.*

*Boom! Boom! BOOM!*

Patrick thought his eardrums would burst from the noise.

Armistead crouched on his feet. "I shouldn't have taken so long to eat," he said. He turned and gripped the boulder with both hands. He peered around it.

*Boom. Boom.*

*Boom! Boom! BOOM!*

"This will go on all day," Armistead said.

"How do you know?" Beth asked.

"The Americans want to force the British to give up," Armistead said.

"But I heard General Cornwallis say he was going to write to George Washington," Patrick said. "Cornwallis would pretend to surrender. Then the British soldiers could escape."

"The British couldn't escape in the storm last night," Armistead said. "That was their last chance."

"Whose side are you on?" Beth asked.

Armistead looked at the cousins, and then he said, "Righ now, the side of safety. We have to get off this battlefield." He gathered his things and waved at them. "Follow close!"

Patrick and Beth reluctantly followed

Armistead into a field of tall weeds. It led to a marsh with bulrushes and tall cat-o'-nine-tails. Patrick's boots stuck in the mud with each step. He felt as if he were walking in a giant tub of gooey chewing gum.

Beth held up the bottom of her long dress. But it still got caked with mud.

They crossed a narrow creek. The rushes grew thicker.

"We're moving away from the Americans," Patrick called out to Armistead.

Armistead pressed on.

Beth came close to Patrick. "Remember the spies we met in Lexington?" Beth asked.

Patrick nodded and said, "There were spies everywhere in the Revolutionary War. Did you see the papers he was shoving in his boot?"

"I saw," Beth said.

"And it looks like he's leading us back to the British side," Patrick said.

James Armistead stopped up ahead. "It's safe now," he said. He pointed in the direction of Yorktown. "If you run that way, you'll find your way home."

"We don't want to go that way!" Patrick said.

Armistead didn't answer. He turned on his heel. He headed back toward the American army.

Patrick watched Armistead cross a small field to the edge of the woods.

"He says he's gathering food for the Americans," Beth said, wringing her hands. "But he is probably spying. He wants to find out the American army's plans. He'll go and tell General Cornwallis."

"Or he's going to deliver the letter that

Cornwallis wrote to fool George Washington,"
Patrick said. "Maybe that's the paper in his
boot."

"What should we do?" Beth asked.

"We have to follow Armistead," Patrick
said. "I bet he'll lead us straight to George
Washington. Then we'll show everyone that
he's a spy."

James Armistead disappeared into the
woods.

"Come on," Patrick said. "We can't lose
him!"

# The French

Beth now hated her long dress. It was heavy with mud along the fringe. Walking was hard work.

She followed Patrick through the woods. Patrick carefully trailed James Armistead. Sometimes Patrick stopped and signaled for Beth to hide behind a tree. He didn't want Armistead to see them.

They crossed another creek. Beth hopped from stone to stone across the rushing water. Her foot slipped. She stumbled into the shallow water. Her dress was now wet and cold and clung to her legs.

Beth struggled up a small ridge. Then down the other side. She joined Patrick standing on the edge of the woods.

A grassy field stretched out before them. The land had been trampled and blown to bits. Everywhere Beth looked she saw signs of war.

For a moment Beth imagined what Yorktown would be like without the war. Would it be peaceful, beautiful, and quiet?

Just then, Beth caught sight of a skunk family. It was as if they were out for a morning stroll. Their tiny black noses sniffed the ground. Their black bodies with white stripes waddled past her.

"Patrick," Beth said, "look!" She pointed

toward the mother and four babies. They shuffled inside a hollow log.

"Poor animals," Patrick said. "I hope a cannonball doesn't smash them."

"I hope a cannonball doesn't smash *us*," Beth said. "Which way now?"

Patrick lifted his hat and wiped his brow. "I wish I knew," he said. "I can't see Armistead anymore."

Beth studied the scene. Row upon row of cannons blasted cannonballs toward Yorktown. Clouds of smoke hung over the field. Groups of soldiers stood at the cannons. Each one was busy loading powder and cannon balls into the cannons. The men fired and loaded them again.

Horses and wagons rattled across the fields. More soldiers marched and drilled. Rows of white tents were everywhere. Beth thought they looked like pigeons sitting on telephone wires.

It was all noise and confusion.

At last Beth spotted Armistead near the center of the field. He was the only man among the Americans wearing a red coat. "There he is!" Beth said to Patrick, pointing.

Beth and Patrick left the woods and entered the green field. They wound their way past tents and cannons toward Armistead.

The spy was chatting with two soldiers. All three men were sitting around a small campfire. Armistead handed each soldier an apple.

*Is he bribing them with apples?* Beth wondered.

Armistead gestured to a tall, white tent nearby. It was larger than all the others.

Armistead gave a slight bow to the two soldiers. Then he walked toward the tent.

"Do you think that's George Washington's tent?" Beth asked.

"It has to be," Patrick said. "Come on. We have to warn him that James Armistead is a spy!"

Patrick ran off. He dodged past soldiers. They didn't seem to notice him at all. Beth gathered her heavy wet skirt and followed.

Patrick raced past the two soldiers by the campfire. Beth was close behind. The two soldiers looked stunned at the arrival of the cousins. Patrick and Beth scooted inside the large tent before the men could stand up.

A large table sat in the middle of the tent. It was covered with maps. Five soldiers stood around the table. Four of them wore white uniforms.

The fifth man was in the center. He wore a white wig with curls on both sides of his face. Gold medals hung from the front of his fancy blue uniform. He looked up at the cousins.

"What is this?" he asked. He spoke in a thick accent. The words came out as *"Wot iz zis?"*

The other officers responded in a language Beth thought was French.

Patrick turned pale. "Where is the man who just came in here?" he asked. "More important, where is George Washington?"

Beth noticed a door-like flap at the back of the tent. It swayed in the breeze. Armistead must have gone out that way.

The French officers jabbered to each other.

"Where is George Washington?" Beth asked again.

"General Washington?" the young Frenchman asked in his thick accent.

Beth was aware of the two guards from the campfire. They were coming up behind her.

Something was terribly wrong. What were the French doing on the American side? Where was General Washington? What had become of James Armistead?

A French officer shouted at the guards. They stepped forward to grab the cousins.

# Skunked

Things happened quickly. The two guards lunged for Patrick and Beth. The cousins dodged them, knocking over the table. Patrick nearly fell. Then Beth grabbed his hand. She pulled him toward the back of the tent. Patrick saw the opening there.

Noises and shouts came from behind them. But the cousins made it outside.

"This way!" Patrick cried. He dropped Beth's hand and raced behind a nearby tent.

"They're coming," Beth gasped.

Patrick peered around the edge of the tent. The two guards ran toward them.

Patrick saw a corral filled with horses. Roughly cut logs had been set up as a fence. "There!" he whispered.

The cousins scrambled over to the corral. The horses stirred as they leaped over the fence. The cousins crouched down and moved among the horses.

One French soldier climbed over the fence to the corral. A horse stepped in front of him, blocking him. The soldier shouted at the horse. It moved with a snort.

The other soldier came into the corral. He was bumped around by the nervous animals.

Patrick and Beth crawled under the other side of the fence. They faced a field. There were woods on the far side.

"To the woods," Patrick said.

They dashed into the field. They ran as fast as they could.

The soldiers shouted at the cousins in French from the corral.

The cousins reached the edge of the woods. Patrick was out of breath.

"They're still chasing us," Beth said, panting.

Three soldiers in white uniforms now ran across the field.

Patrick knew they couldn't outrun them much longer. He needed a plan. His eye went to the fallen log he'd seen before. He ran over to it.

"We have to keep going," Beth said.

He pointed to a large tree. "Hide behind that," he said. "When I say 'run' then run as fast as you can into the woods."

Patrick went to the back end of the fallen log. He grabbed a stick and began to beat on the top. Patrick watched the edge of the woods for the soldiers.

Beth looked confused. "What are you doing?" she shouted.

"I'm trying to get the skunks out," Patrick said.

Beth blinked. "Why didn't you say so?" she asked. "But pounding won't help."

"Then how do we get them out?" he asked.

Beth frowned. Then her face lit up. "Skunks hate strange noises." She took the fife out of her pocket. She blew a high-pitched note. Nothing happened.

One of the soldiers reached the woods. He saw Patrick and Beth.

Patrick looked at Beth in panic. He jumped

on top of the log and stomped his feet. He hoped the skunks hadn't left the log.

The French soldier stopped. He looked puzzled by the cousins' strange behavior. He called out to them in French.

Beth changed her fingering on the fife. "Stop jumping," she said. "You may be scaring them."

"I thought that was the point," Patrick said.

Beth knelt down at the back opening of the log. She blew another note. This one was louder and off-key.

The other two soldiers entered the woods. The first soldier held up his hand to stop them. He said something in French. The three men slowly walked toward the cousins.

Patrick watched the soldiers. They spoke calmly. They seemed to be coaxing the cousins to come to them.

"They're getting closer," Patrick said.

Beth kept blowing on the fife.

The soldiers were only a few feet away now. Patrick worried they might jump at them. He jumped off the log and backed toward Beth. "Get ready to run," he said.

Just then, the skunks rushed out of the front opening of the log. They ran

toward the Frenchmen. Their black-and-white fluffy tails were raised high.

"Yiii," the first French soldier cried out. He staggered into the other two men.

"Moo-fet! Moo-fet!" the second soldier shouted. Patrick guessed the soldier was shouting the French word for skunk.

The three men stumbled back, tripping over each other.

The skunks ran at them.

The three soldiers ran out of the woods.

# Explosion!

"That did the trick," Patrick said.

Beth laughed.

Then the skunks turned toward them. The mother skunk came close and stamped her paws on the ground.

"Uh-oh," Beth said. "I think they want their log back."

The cousins backed away from the skunks. Beth was about to turn and run.

Then *boom!* A cannonball landed nearby.

Beth saw leaves and bushes fly upward.
Sand rained down on the cousins. The
skunks bolted into the thicket.

"Run!" Patrick shouted. The cousins ran
deeper into the woods.

Beth saw a thicket that made a shelter
like a tent. The opening was too small for
an adult. But a child could fit. She crawled
inside.

The floor was covered with leaves, twigs,
and coarse sand. There was a sandpile in
the back. But there was enough flat area to
sit down.

*Patrick crawled inside after her.* "This . . .
feels . . . safe," he said between breaths.

Beth's breathing slowed. She said, "I'm
confused. What happened in the tent? Why
are the French here?"

"I think I remember something about the

French," Patrick said. "They didn't want England to get too powerful. So they helped the Americans in the Revolutionary War."

"Then why did we run from them?" she asked.

"Because they thought we were spies," Patrick said.

"Not again," Beth said with a groan. "Why do people always think we're spies or slaves or stowaways?"

"Because we usually are," Patrick said. All of a sudden, he slapped his leg. "Ants!"

Just then Beth felt a sting on her hand. She looked at it. There was a red bump near her thumb. There was also a large red ant.

"Ouch!" she cried. "I'm getting out of here!"

She brushed the ant off. And then she pushed past Patrick and crawled out of the opening. She stood and shook the skirt of her dress. "Get off, you little pests," she said.

She put her hand inside her pocket. The fife was gone.

Patrick's head and shoulders poked out of the hole. But he was still on his hands and knees.

"Patrick," she said, "I dropped my fife. Is it in there?"

"Let me see," he said. He backed up and disappeared into the shelter. There was a pause. Then Beth heard leaves rustling.

Finally Patrick said, "Yes. I have it." Patrick's hand appeared with the fife.

Beth grabbed it. "Thanks," she said. "Now get out of there. Or you'll be bit."

"What does it mean when a skunk stomps its feet?" he asked.

"It's mad," Beth said. "Why?"

"The skunks are in here," Patrick said.

"The mother is stomping her foot. But she doesn't look mad. The babies are eating ants."

"That must be so cute!" Beth said. She tried to peek inside. But Patrick's body still blocked the opening. "What's happening?"

"The mother—" Patrick said.

"The mother what?" Beth asked

"Ahhh!" Patrick screamed.

Beth helped Patrick remove his blue jacket and hat. They had taken most of the spray. She felt bad for him.

Beth's eyes stung so badly she was crying. And she hadn't even been sprayed. The stench also burned the inside of her nose. It smelled stronger than a cat's dirty litter box.

She studied Patrick's face. It was red and

blotchty. His eyes were almost swollen shut.

"Let's find some water," he said. "I need to wash off this gross smell. Plus, it burns." He pulled the delivery map out of his pocket.

He handed it to Beth. "You read it."

Beth rolled out the map and held the edges. "Wormley Creek is nearby," she said. "It'll be shallow enough for you to bathe in."

The cousins walked through the woods. The shelling seemed mostly to the left. Beth figured that was the direction of Yorktown. If they stayed to the right they would reach the creek.

The woods thinned out to a large field. Cannons fired to the left. Suddenly there were explosions to the right.

"They're on both sides!" Beth cried out.

"Let's run for it," Patrick said and dashed forward.

"Wait for me!" she cried.

Directly ahead was the river. They saw what was left of the British ships there. Suddenly one of the larger ships burst into flames. Patrick saw British soldiers in red coats jumping from the sides. Billows of black smoke rose to the blue sky.

*Kaboom. KABOOM!* Now the burning ship exploded. The whole ground shook. Large pieces of wood flew up into the air.

The impact caused Patrick to stumble. Beth reached out to steady him. He lost his footing and fell forward, dragging Beth with him.

Beth lost Patrick's hand. They tumbled head over heels down, down, down into a deep trench. The sandy soil flew into Beth's mouth. Mud covered her eyes. She had no idea what was happening.

# The Trench

Patrick opened his eyes. He was staring up at Beth. She was leaning over him. Her face was muddy. So was the rest of her.

"Are you all right?" Beth asked. She looked worried.

Patrick shook his head. He sat up and spit the dirt out of his mouth. The back of his head was sore from the fall.

Patrick looked around. They were at the bottom of a long trench. It stretched away around curves on both sides of them.

"This must be one of the trenches they use for cover," Patrick said.

"Who uses it?" Beth asked. "The British or the Americans?"

Patrick stood and tried to climb up the dirt sides of the trench. The sandy soil was loose and slippery. He got enough of a footing to peek over the top edge. Then he slid down to the bottom again.

"Yorktown and the river are that way," Patrick said. He pointed down the trench to their left. "And the tents and cannons are that way." Next he pointed to the right. "And probably behind us."

Beth shook the dirt off of her skirt. Then she wrinkled her nose. "How do we get to some water?" she asked. "You still smell to high heaven."

"It's safe from gunfire down here," Patrick said. "And I saw a wooden wall farther along the trench. It's probably a fort. I didn't see anyone nearby."

"I'll follow you," Beth said.

The cousins followed the trench. The dirt walls were high above their heads on both sides of them. The path was snakelike as it wound this way and that.

*Boom! Boom! Boom!* The cannons made a steady noise from above them.

They reached the wall of wooden beams. It was a makeshift fort with a ladder. There was a ledge along the top for guards to watch the enemy.

"It's facing the Americans," Beth said.

"That means it was left here by the British," Patrick said. He tested the ladder and climbed up.

"Be careful," Beth said.

He crouched on the upper shelf and peeked over the top.

"Uh-oh!" he called out. Hundreds of soldiers in blue uniforms marched in rows. They carried rifles with bayonets fixed at the end. The men were following wheeled cannons.

"What's wrong?" Beth asked.

"We're closer to the cannons," Patrick called down to her. "Or they're getting closer to us!"

"What do you mean?" she said.

Patrick watched as the rows of soldiers suddenly turned. Now they were marching toward the trench!

"Oh no," he said in a low voice.

Suddenly the soldiers pointed their rifles forward and started running. One of them shouted, "Rush on, boys!"

"They're charging this way!" Patrick cried. He slid down the ladder to Beth. "Back the way we came! Hurry!"

Patrick and Beth turned and ran back down the trench. Behind them, soldiers poured into the trench opening.

Beth's heavy wet skirt whipped against her legs. As the cousins ran, the soldiers sounded farther behind them. Rifle shots were fired. She hoped they weren't shooting at her.

Patrick was just ahead of her.

Beth looked back down the trench and couldn't see anything. The sounds of war seemed farther off.

"Patrick," she cried. "Wait!"

Patrick slowed.

"Give me a boost?" she asked.

Patrick knelt on one knee. The other was bent.

Beth used his bent leg as a stair. She stuck her head above the trench. She looked around.

"The soldiers have climbed out a nearby trench," she told Patrick. "They're running toward Yorktown."

"Do you see water?" Patrick asked.

Beth looked around the field. She saw Wormley Creek. No one seemed to be fighting near it. "Yes, the creek is nearby," she said.

"Can you believe this?" Patrick said angrily. "We're stuck between two sides in a war. And I smell like skunk!"

Beth hopped off Patrick's knee.

Patrick stood up. "Sorry," he said. "I don't

want to be a grouch. But my skin hurts." He scratched at his white shirt.

"We have to get you cleaned up," Beth said.

They followed the trench back to where it was closest to the creek. They climbed out and lay down on the grass. They looked around to make sure it was safe. Then they stood and ran to a nearby grove of trees.

The grove was littered like a junkyard. Parts of a broken wagon sat off to the side. The remains of campfires dotted the ground. Rubbish and bits of white cloth hung from the sides of trees. Holes made by cannon shells pocked the earth. Sides of trees were splintered.

Beth saw a wooden trunk next to the wagon. It was turned up on one end.

Patrick came up next to her. "What's all that stuff?" he asked.

Beth rummaged around inside the trunk. She picked up a white shirt. "This might fit," she said.

"Why would they have extra clothes out here?" Patrick asked.

"I think this was a storage area," Beth said. "They have more uniforms than soldiers now." The sad thought made her want to end the war even more.

Patrick pointed with his toe at something round. It looked like a drum.

Beth pulled out a red jacket that was covered by a tarp. "Maybe it's a drummer boy's uniform," she said.

"Oh, no," Patrick said. "I'm not putting that on. I can't look like one of the redcoats. The Americans will shoot me!"

Beth pointed to the creek nearby. "Stop complaining and go wash," she said.

# Deserters

Patrick found a section of the creek covered with bushes. They were thick enough to give him privacy. He took off his clothes and washed as well as he could.

Afterward Patrick's chest was still red and itchy from the skunk spray. And he still smelled bad.

Cannon fire and rifle shots sounded in the distance.

"Hurry!" Beth said from afar.

Patrick climbed out of the creek. He put on the clothes she'd found. "They'll think I'm a spy!" Patrick said.

"Then you'll be the smelliest spy ever," Beth said.

"That's not funny," Patrick said, grumbling. He imagined meeting George Washington. The general would think he was a smelly redcoat.

Patrick heard a rustling from the other side of the bushes. Beth said something, but it was muffled.

Patrick finished dressing and stepped out. He was dressed in the white shirt and the bright-red jacket of a British drummer boy.

"Well? How do I look?" he asked.

Beth stood in front of him. Behind her was James Armistead. The spy's hand was pressed over her mouth. He wore the red jacket and pants he'd had on before. The same black hat with white-and-purple flowers sat on his head. The satchel over his shoulder hung down by his side.

"You changed your coat," Armistead said.

Patrick's mind raced with what to do. His mind was blank. What *could* he do?

Armistead released his hand from Beth's mouth. But he held onto her collar so she couldn't run away.

Beth looked at Patrick helplessly.

"Sprayed by a skunk?" Armistead asked. "My guess is that your skin is really red and sore by now."

Patrick nodded. "What about it?" he asked.

"You want to use some jewelweed," Armistead said. "It grows by the creek. It'll cure the itch and pain."

Patrick crossed his arms. He was suspicious. "You're a spy," he said. "Why would you help us?"

"You think I'm a spy?" Armistead said with a small laugh. "And what are the two of you? One minute I see you in General Cornwallis's hideout. The next I see you sneaking over to the other side. Now he's got a British uniform on."

"We're not British Loyalists," Beth said.

"It doesn't really matter," Armistead said. "You have to get away from here. The French and American troops are coming through. Stay with me, and you'll be all right."

Patrick and Beth looked at one another. *Should we trust him?* Beth's expression asked.

"You could have easily turned us in earlier," Patrick said. "But you didn't. And you could take her as prisoner now. But you aren't going to."

Beth said, "We can come a little way with you."

Armistead let go of Beth's collar. "Fair enough," he said. "Now let's find that jewelweed for your skunk skin."

Patrick felt instant relief when the jewelweed touched his sore skin. The skunk smell seemed to fade, too.

Patrick, Beth, and Armistead then left the creek area. Armistead zigzagged his way toward the river. Patrick and Beth followed along. Beth frowned the whole way but didn't speak.

Patrick knew they were headed in the direction of Yorktown again. He wished he had a plan for escape. But, at the moment, he felt lost. More than that, he worried about wandering into the line of fire.

Patrick soon recognized the area. They were returning to General Cornwallis's cave.

"You tricked us!" Patrick cried.

"You're not nice," Beth said.

"Be patient, children," Armistead said. "It will work out yet."

Armistead guided the cousins inside the cave. The general was talking with Officer Mudge. General Cornwallis looked up.

"Armistead!" General Cornwallis said. "Where have you been?"

Armistead gave a slight bow. "I took your letter to the Americans," he said. "I did as you instructed."

Patrick scowled. So it was true. Armistead was part of the general's scheme.

General Cornwallis frowned. "Yet they still

fire at us," he said. "The cannons do not stop. Why?"

"They didn't believe you," Armistead said. "They knew you were trying to delay them. They knew you might try to escape. And then counterattack."

"The weather put an end to that plan," Officer Mudge said with a snort.

Hearing Officer Mudge snort reminded Patrick about the handkerchief. He worried it might be inside his blue coat. He reached into his pants pocket. He sighed with relief. The handkerchief was there.

"Fate continues to work against me," the general said. He clasped his hands behind his back. He paced a few steps.

"It's not for me to say what fate does," Armistead said.

"Why have you brought these children?"

Officer Mudge asked. "Isn't this a laundry girl? And what is this boy?"

"He smells of skunk," the general said with a sniff.

"He is a drummer boy," Armistead said.

Patrick said, "I'm not—"

Armistead put a hand on Patrick's shoulder to silence him.

"Are we in need of a drummer boy?" the general asked.

"For the surrender," Armistead said.

The general looked at Armistead with sad eyes.

Officer Mudge shook his head. "Why should we surrender?" he asked.

"I have seen the strength of your enemies," Armistead said. "You're fighting the combined forces of the Continental army and the French. General Washington leads one. General Lafayette leads the other."

*Lafayette!* Patrick thought and felt stupid. Lafayette was the young officer with the curls. He was the Frenchman in the tent.

"You cannot win against them," Armistead said.

"Why should we believe you?" Officer Mudge asked.

"Because you promised me freedom if you win," Armistead said. "I have no reason to lie."

Armistead gestured to the cousins. "Ask them," he said. "They've seen what I've seen."

Officer Mudge and the general looked at the cousins.

"It's true," Patrick said. "You can't win. You're surrounded. They have plenty of cannonballs. There's food and supplies."

Beth added, "The only way out is to sprout

wings and fly."

Armistead took a step toward the general. His hands reached out. "Please, General Cornwallis," he said. "Save your men from being killed."

"Get out," the general said with a wave of his hand. "Leave me to consider our plans."

Armistead and the cousins stepped out of the cave.

They startled a redcoat who had been listening.

"Surrender?" he asked softly.

"You believe you should keep fighting?" Armistead asked him.

"Not at all," the redcoat said. "It would be a relief to stop now. I haven't eaten for two days."

The redcoat stood on guard at the cave entrance. He had a mournful look.

"I don't get it," Patrick said to Armistead. "Are you a spy or not?"

Armistead faced Patrick and Beth. He smiled like a cat. "There is a reason the French and Americans didn't believe Cornwallis's letter," he said. "It was because *I told them not to.* And this morning I told Lafayette how desperate the British troops have become."

Beth gasped. "So you're a spy for the Americans?" she asked.

James Armistead gave a small shrug. "I'm a servant to freedom," he said.

A moment later Officer Mudge emerged from the cave. He seemed unhappy. "Get your things," he said to Patrick.

"What things?" Patrick asked.

"You're a drummer boy, aren't you?" he snapped.

Patrick looked to Armistead for help. The spy nodded. Patrick knew he had to go along with the plan.

Officer Mudge called to the redcoat on guard. "Get this boy a drum and a pair of drumsticks," he said. "On the double."

The soldier saluted; then he left.

"I'll want someone who plays the fife," the officer said.

Beth looked startled. She fumbled in her pocket. She quickly pulled out the fife that Whit had given her. "Like this one?" she asked.

"That'll do," Officer Mudge said.

"What does this mean?" Armistead asked.

"General Cornwallis has taken you at your word," Officer Mudge said. "He is going to surrender."

# Blindfolded

Beth took in a quick breath. Patrick was astonished. This was an answer to their prayers.

"It pains me to admit this," Officer Mudge said. "The British army must surrender. We have lost many, many lives in this wasted fight."

Office Mudge's eyes locked on Patrick and Beth. The soldier said, "Now I need a drummer boy and fife player. They are to climb to the top of the ridge. We must tell the Americans what we have decided."

"But I don't know how to play the drums," Patrick said.

"You weary me!" Officer Mudge said. "I don't give a twopence if you can play. I want you to make noise."

The redcoat returned with a drum. He fit the straps on Patrick's back. Then he hung the heavy drum in front. He pushed two drumsticks into Patrick's hands.

"The time has come," Officer Mudge said.

"You will go with them?" Armistead asked.

"It is my duty," Officer Mudge said.

"What may I do?" Armistead asked.

"Your services will no longer be needed," Officer Mudge said to Armistead. "Go and hope to find freedom in another time and another place."

Armistead gave a slight bow to the officer. Then he faced Patrick and Beth and gave another bow. He turned and walked away.

"Follow me," Officer Mudge said.

The cousins obeyed. They followed Officer Mudge along the river's edge. Then they followed him along a trail through the bluffs. Officer Mudge led them past dugouts filled with British soldiers. Most of them looked tired and sick.

"How will the Americans know not to shoot us?" Patrick asked Officer Mudge.

"They won't," the officer said. They marched on.

Patrick leaned toward Beth. "You can't come," he said in a serious tone. "It's too dangerous."

"I *have* to come," Beth said. She held up her fife. "Mr. Whittaker gave this to me to use. It has to be for this."

Patrick shook his head. Everything was turning out wrong. He thought he was going to meet George Washington. Instead he was helping the British surrender.

They reached a thick dirt wall. Soldiers crouched down behind it. Sharp-pointed logs stuck out the other side.

*Boom! Boom! Boom!* The noise of the cannons was loud and close. Patrick felt as if the whole world was exploding around them. The sharp smell of burning powder stung his nose.

Officer Mudge motioned for the cousins to march in front of him. A trail led up to the top of the dirt wall.

Patrick turned to Beth again. "Stay here," he said. "Please!"

She shook her head.

Patrick and Beth marched up the trail. Officer Mudge walked slightly behind them.

Patrick held the drumsticks tight. The pressure made his fingers turn white. He saw Beth lift the fife to her lips beside him. Her hands shook.

Patrick banged on the drums. Left. Right. Left. Right. *Rat-a-tat-tat. Rat-a-tat-tat.*

Beth blew into the hole of the fife. But her breath came in nervous gasps. It was hard to hear a single note.

A row of British soldiers stood at the bottom of the dirt wall. Some saluted them, others wept.

Officer Mudge directed Patrick and Beth to a set of makeshift stairs. They followed the stairs to the top of the dirt wall.

Patrick looked at the field below. A long

line of cannons pointed straight at him
and Beth. Clouds of smoke surrounded the
cannons.

Patrick saw Officer Mudge reach into his
pocket. Officer Mudge muttered something
and then reached into his other pocket.

"I need something white!" he cried out.
"I've forgotten my handkerchief!"

Patrick now understood. This was
exactly where he and Beth were supposed
to be. The two gifts were for this moment.
Patrick grabbed the handkerchief that Mr.
Whittaker had given him. He handed it to
Officer Mudge.

A nearby redcoat waved a British flag that
was on a pole. Officer Mudge took the pole.
He stripped off the flag. Then he tied the
handkerchief to it.

Officer Mudge nodded his gratitude to

Patrick and the redcoat. The soldier then raised the pole and waved the handkerchief in the air. Patrick beat a slow rhythm on the drums. Beth played the fife next to him.

The cannons fell silent one at a time. Shouts came from the American side. And then those also stopped.

Officer Mudge continued to wave the handkerchief in the air.

Finally, Patrick's drum and Beth's fife were the only sounds in the open field. They stepped ahead of Officer Mudge.

An American soldier separated himself from the line of cannons in front of them. He wore a buckskin coat.

Patrick stopped playing the drum. Beth lowered her fife. She clutched it close to her.

The air was still and silent. It was as if the whole world was holding its breath.

The American soldier ran up and approached the bottom of the dirt wall.

"What is your message?" the soldier asked.

"I wish to offer terms of surrender," Officer Mudge cried down to him. "Take me to your commanding officer."

The soldier scrambled up the dirt wall. He squeezed through the pointed logs. He stood next to Patrick.

"Blindfolds," he said to Officer Mudge.

Officer Mudge called out to the British soldiers standing at the bottom of the wall. "I need blindfolds!"

Patrick heard the sound of ripping fabric. Then strips of white cloth were handed up to the officer. The soldier wearing the buckskin coat used Patrick's handkerchief as a blindfold for Officer Mudge. Then he used the other strips to blindfold Beth and Patrick.

"We're on your side," Beth whispered to the man in buckskin.

"You are now," the man whispered back.

Patrick didn't like not being able to see. He put both drumsticks in one hand. He reached out to grab Beth's hand with his other.

"Come on," the soldier said in a gruff voice. He guided Patrick by the shoulder and led them away.

# 15

# *Your Excellency*

Beth felt grateful for Patrick's hand. It was hard to walk wearing a blindfold. Her skirt was damp and heavy with mud. She stumbled several times but didn't fall. Patrick helped her stay on her feet.

She heard men's voices talking quietly as they walked past. She smelled the smoke from the cannons. A horse whinnied.

The sounds changed from the open battlefield to what she imagined was an enclosed camp. She heard the rustle of canvas and fabric. A campfire crackled.

Then she was guided into a tent. Patrick let go of her hand. Her blindfold was pulled off. She was standing next to Patrick and Officer Mudge. The soldier in the buckskin coat was in front of them. He spoke softly to someone and then stepped aside.

Several soldiers in blue uniforms stood in a line ahead of them. One was taller than the others. His white hair was pulled back in a ponytail. He wore a large blue hat in the shape of a triangle. His face was pleasant, but his mouth seemed set in a frown. He wore a long blue jacket with gold trim along the front, bottom, and sleeves.

The jacket had fancy gold fringe on the shoulders. His vest and pants were white, and he wore tall black boots. A thin sword hung at his side.

Beth knew him from all the paintings and engravings she'd seen. It was George Washington.

● ● ●

*George Washington!* Patrick thought and held back a gasp. He hardly knew how to feel. He was looking at the future first president of the United States face-to-face. All he could do was grin.

Patrick looked at Beth. She had tears in her eyes. *Typical girl*, he thought.

"Your Excellency," the soldier in the buckskin coat said. "General Cornwallis wants to offer terms of surrender. He wishes for officials from both sides to meet. He suggests the Moore farm as the place to discuss the terms."

Washington's frown slowly shaped into a

smile. He took a deep breath and stood even taller.

"We are glad to stop the loss of blood," he said. "We will call a truce for two hours while your general writes a formal proposal."

He motioned to the soldier in the buckskin coat. "Blindfold them again," he said.

"Wait!" Patrick said, stepping forward. "We're not British. We're Americans. We belong here."

The soldier in the buckskin coat tied the blindfold over Officer Mudge's eyes.

"I don't know what the boy is talking about," Officer Mudge said. "They have been with us as laundry workers. Unless they are your spies."

"We do not use children as spies," George Washington said.

"Please don't send us back, Mr. President!" Beth cried.

All the men looked at Beth with surprised expressions.

"What did you call me?" Washington asked.

"I meant *general*," Beth said, blushing.

Just then Beth heard footsteps. They were running toward them from outside. Men's loud voices came close.

"What is happening?" a voice asked with a thick French accent. The young soldier in the fancy blue jacket stood in the tent entryway. Beth now recognized him as Lafayette.

"Will someone tell me what is going on?" Officer Mudge said. He was still blindfolded.

George Washington held up his hand. It was a signal for everyone to be quiet. Then he pointed to Officer Mudge. "This officer does not need a drum or fife," George Washington said. "He is to return to General Cornwallis with no fanfare." He turned to the soldier in the buckskin coat. "Take him back."

The soldier led Officer Mudge away.

Nobody spoke until he was gone.

"General Lafayette!" Washington said suddenly. His tone was filled with joy. "The British have surrendered!"

"Huzzah! Huzzah!" Lafayette cried.

"This is all because of my friend James Armistead," Lafayette said. "He risked his life to bring us valuable information."

"Where is he?" General Washington asked.

"We left him outside of Cornwallis's hideout," Patrick said. "We thought he was a spy for the British!"

Lafayette looked at the cousins. "Ah yes!"

he said. "You are the mysterious children. You appeared in my tent this morning. We were afraid you would ruin our plans for the surrender."

"How do I know you are not spies?" Washington asked.

"We aren't," Beth said to the general. "We've been trying to find you to tell you the British plans for escape."

"But we prayed. And God used the storm to keep them from escaping," Patrick said.

The general looked at Patrick with a puzzled expression.

Patrick said, "We're not spies. But I'm still not sure about Armistead."

General Washington put his hand on Patrick's shoulder. "James Armistead has been a double agent," Washington said. "He has had a very dangerous job. He has

served the cause of freedom well."

Beth remembered that Armistead had used those words to describe himself.

"How do you know who to trust?" Patrick asked.

"In war, we trust only God Himself," Washington said. "After Benedict Arnold and Dr. Church of the Provincial Congress—"

"We met Dr. Church in Concord," Patrick said. "We suspected him right away."

"Concord?" Washington said, surprised. "You children are very far from home."

"You have no idea," Beth said softly.

"General, we need to make plans for the British surrender," Lafayette reminded Washington.

The general nodded. He said, "Our first task is to thank God for bringing this day to pass. It's been a long, hard war. We have reached this moment only by His gracious hand."

George Washington took off his hat and knelt on one knee. Lafayette knelt next to him. The other officers knelt where they were.

Beth and Patrick knelt down too. Beth closed her eyes.

"Almighty God," Washington said. "We are grateful for your benefits. We humbly ask for your protection and favor. You are the great Lord and Ruler of Nations. Amen."

"Amen," Beth said along with the others.

They all stood.

From outside the tent, Beth heard a familiar whirring sound. The Imagination Station was waiting for them.

Patrick reached out to shake George Washington's hand. "Thank you for leading our country, Your Excellency," Patrick said.

Washington's eyes twinkled. "Please see my second-in-command. He will arrange a bath and a change of clothes."

"Thank you," Patrick said. "But I have fresh clothes waiting for me somewhere else."

General Washington smiled and turned to the other officers. "We have work to do," he said.

Patrick saluted General Lafayette. "Thank you for your help, General. One day America will return the favor."

"I will look forward to that," Lafayette said. Then he saluted the cousins.

Beth and Patrick walked out of the tent. The Imagination Station waited for them next to a lone tree. The cousins climbed in.

Patrick pushed the red button.

# 16

# *Whit's End*

Patrick jumped out of the Imagination Station. "Shake my hand, Whit!" he cried. "Shake my hand!"

Whit was seated at his workbench. He reached out to shake Patrick's hand.

Patrick was excited. He said, "You just shook the hand that shook the hand of the first president of the United States!"

"So you met George Washington after all," Whit said, grinning.

"It took a while," Beth said. "We seemed to be in all the wrong places."

"But then we saw him!" Patrick said. He was glad it finally happened.

"We even *prayed* with him," Beth said. "I'm really glad he believed in God."

"He certainly did," Whit said. "As president he published a proclamation. It declared a day of thanksgiving and prayer. He asked God to forgive the nation's sins. He asked for God's help so our government would be wise and kind."

"A lot of the people we met during the Revolutionary War were Christians," Patrick said.

Whit nodded. He picked up a big Bible from his workbench. It had gold lettering on the outside and old yellow pages inside.

"You remember this," he said.

"It's your family's Bible from Colonial times," Beth said.

Whit nodded. "The Founding Fathers wrote documents and laws for our country," he said. "They were based on truths found in the Bible."

Patrick was quiet for a moment. He thought of James Forten, who had been threatened with slavery. And James

Armistead, who had been a slave. Yet both served the country before it figured out that slavery was wrong. "The Founding Fathers didn't get everything right," he said quietly.

Whit placed his hand on the Bible. He said, "It's true. We live in a sinful world. Sometimes good men and women who hope to do right still fail. That's why we have to turn to our Bibles and our faith and the power of prayer to help them."

"But you fooled us," Patrick said.

"How?" Whit asked.

"I hoped we would do something important for George Washington," Patrick said.

"But we spent most of our time helping the British," Beth added.

"You helped the British to surrender," Whit reminded him. "Don't you think that was important?"

Patrick thought about it. "Yeah, I guess so."

"The American and French armies had the British cornered," Whit said. "But victory for one side and defeat for the other didn't come easily. Everyone had to play their parts."

"And we played ours!" Beth said, then lifted an eyebrow. "Though we didn't know we were playing it until the end."

"Which is how history often works," Whit said. "We play our parts by faith without knowing how things will turn out."

Now Patrick felt excited again. "I can't wait to go to Boston with Grandma," he said. "All that history will mean more because it came alive for us."

Whit smiled. "That's why I built the Imagination Station," he said, "Come back when you're ready for a new adventure."

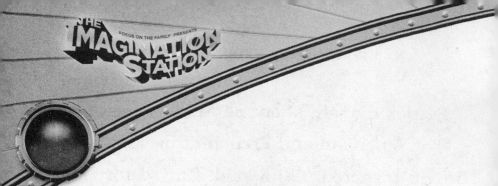

# Secret Word Puzzle

Americans used guns and cannons to fight
in the Revolutionary War. But many leaders
used three other powerful weapons to win the
fight for freedom. You can find out what these
weapons are. Start with the letter P at the
top of the circle. Move in the direction of the
arrows. Write down every other letter, in order,
on the lines and inside the boxes. The secret
word will appear inside the boxes.

P _rayer, the Bible,_

_and_ ☐F☐ ☐a☐ ☐i☐ ☐t☐ ☐h☐

_in Jesus._

## Secret Word Puzzle

*Go to TheImaginationStation.com. Find the cover of this book. Click on "Secret Word." Type in the correct answer, and you'll receive a prize.*

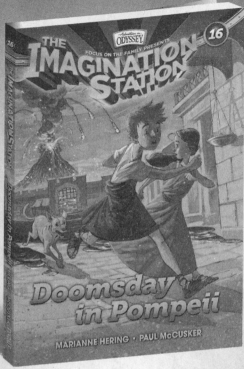